John Fox

Hell fer Sartain

John Fox

Hell fer Sartain

ISBN/EAN: 9783744670920

Printed in Europe, USA, Canada, Australia, Japan

Cover: Foto ©Andreas Hilbeck / pixelio.de

More available books at **www.hansebooks.com**

"HELL FER SARTAIN"

AND OTHER STORIES

BY

JOHN FOX, Jr.
AUTHOR OF
"A CUMBERLAND VENDETTA" ETC.

NEW YORK
HARPER & BROTHERS PUBLISHERS
1897

TO
MY BROTHER
JAMES

AUTHOR'S NOTE

These stories were originally published in *Harper's Weekly*, *The Century*, *Southern Magazine*, and *The Graphic*, London.

"Hell fer Sartain," included in "A Cumberland Vendetta, and Other Stories," is reprinted here, because it is one of the series of similar monologues contained in this volume.

CONTENTS

ON HELL-FER-SARTAIN CREEK

THAR was a dancin'-party Christmas night on "Hell fer Sartain." Jes tu'n up the fust crick beyond the bend thar, an' climb onto a stump, an' holler about *once*, an' you'll see how the name come. Stranger, hit's *hell* fer sartain! Well, Rich Harp was thar from the head-waters, an' Harve Hall toted Nance Osborn clean across the Cumberlan'. Fust one ud swing Nance, an' then t'other. Then they'd take a pull out'n the same bottle o' moonshine, an'—fust one an' then t'other—they'd swing her

3

agin. An' Abe Shivers a-settin' thar by the fire a-bitin' his thumbs!

Well, things was sorter whoopin', when somebody ups an' tells Harve that Rich had said somep'n' agin Nance an' him, an' somebody ups an' tells Rich that Harve had said somep'n' agin Nance an' *him*. In a minute, stranger, hit was like two wild-cats in thar. Folks got 'em parted, though, but thar was no more a-swingin' of Nance that night. Harve toted her back over the Cumberlan', an' Rich's kinsfolks tuk him up " Hell fer Sartain "; but Rich got loose, an' lit out lickety-split fer Nance Osborn's. He knowed Harve lived too fer over Black Mountain to go home that night, an' he rid right across the river an' up to Nance's house, an' hollered fer Harve. Harve poked his head

4

out'n the loft — he knowed whut was wanted—an' Harve says, " Uh, come in hych an' go to bed. Hit's too late !" An' Rich seed him a-gapin' like a chicken, an' in he walked, stumblin' might' nigh agin the bed whar Nance was a-layin', listenin' an' not sayin' a word.

Stranger, them two fellers slept together plum frien'ly, an' they et together plum frien'ly next mornin', an' they sa'ntered down to the grocery plum frien'ly. An' Rich says, " Harve," says he, " let's have a drink." " All right, Rich," says Harve. An' Rich says, " Harve," says he, " you go out'n that door an' I'll go out'n this door." " All right, Rich," says Harve, an' out they walked, steady, an' thar was two shoots shot, an' Rich an' Harve both drapped, an' in ten minutes they was stretched out on Nance's bed an' Nance was a-lopin' away fer the yarb doctor.

The gal nussed 'em both plum faithful. Rich didn't hev much to say, an' Harve didn't hev much to say. Nance was sorter quiet, an' Nance's mammy, ole Nance, jes grinned. Folks come in to ax atter 'em right peart. Abe Shivers come cl'ar 'cross the river—powerful frien'ly—an' ever' time Nance ud walk out to the fence with him. One time she didn't come back, an' ole Nance fotched the boys thar dinner, an' ole Nance fotched thar supper, an' then Rich he axed whut was the matter with young Nance. An' ole Nance jes snorted. Atter a while Rich says: " Harve," says he, " who tol' you that I said that word agin you an' Nance?" " Abe Shivers," says Harve. " An' who tol' you," says Harve, "that I said that word agin Nance an' *you?*" "Abe Shivers," says Rich. An' both says, "Well, damn me!" An' Rich tu'ned right over an' begun pullin' straws out'n the bed. He got two out, an' he bit one off, an' he says: "Harve," says he, "I reckon we better draw fer him. The shortes' gits him." An' they drawed. Well, nobody ever knowed which got the shortes' straw, stranger, but—

Thar'll be a dancin'-party comin' Christmas night on "Hell fer Sartain." Rich Harp 'll be thar from the headwaters. Harve Hall's a-goin' to tote the Widder Shivers clean across the Cumberlan'. Fust one 'll swing Nance, an' then t'other. Then they'll take a pull out'n the same bottle o' moonshine, an'—fust one an' then t'other—

they'll swing her agin, jes the same.
Abe won't be thar. He's a-settin' by
a bigger fire, I reckon (ef he ain't in
it), a-bitin' his thumbs!

THROUGH THE GAP

WHEN thistles go adrift, the sun sets down the valley between the hills; when snow comes, it goes down behind the Cumberland and streams through a great fissure that people call the Gap. Then the last light drenches the parson's cottage under Imboden Hill, and leaves an after-glow of glory on a majestic heap that lies against the east. Sometimes it spans the Gap with a rainbow.

Strange people and strange tales come through this Gap from the Kentucky hills. Through it came these two, late one day—a man and a woman — afoot. I met them at the footbridge over Roaring Fork.

"Is thar a preacher anywhar aroun' hyeh?" he asked. I pointed to the cottage under Imboden Hill. The girl flushed slightly and turned her head away with a rather unhappy smile. Without a word, the mountaineer led the way towards town. A moment more and a half-breed Malungian passed me on the bridge and followed them.

At dusk the next day I saw the mountaineer chopping wood at a shanty under a clump of rhododendron on the river-bank. The girl was cooking supper inside. The day following he was at work on the railroad, and on

Sunday, after church, I saw the parson. The two had not been to him. Only that afternoon the mountaineer was on the bridge with another woman, hideously rouged and with scarlet ribbons fluttering from her bonnet. Passing on by the shanty, I saw the Malungian talking to the girl. She apparently paid no heed to him until, just as he was moving away, he said something mockingly, and with a nod of his head back towards the bridge. She did not look up even then, but her face got hard and white, and, looking back from the road, I saw her slipping through the bushes into the dry bed of the creek, to make sure that what the half-breed told her was true.

The two men were working side by side on the railroad when I saw them

again, but on the first pay-day the doctor was called to attend the Malungian, whose head was split open with
a shovel. I was one of two who went
out to arrest his assailant, and I had
no need to ask who he was. The
mountaineer was a devil, the foreman
said, and I had to club him with a
pistol-butt before he would give in.
He said he would get even with me;
but they all say that, and I paid no
attention to the threat. For a week he
was kept in the calaboose, and when I
passed the shanty just after he was
sent to the county-seat for trial, I
found it empty. The Malungian, too,
was gone. Within a fortnight the
mountaineer was in the door of the
shanty again. Having no accuser, he
had been discharged. He went back

14

to his work, and if he opened his lips I never knew. Every day I saw him at work, and he never failed to give me a surly look. Every dusk I saw him in his door-way, waiting, and I could guess for what. It was easy to believe that the stern purpose in his face would make its way through space and draw her to him again. And she did come back one day. I had just limped down the mountain with a sprained ankle. A crowd of women was gathered at the edge of the woods, looking with all their eyes to the shanty on the river-bank. The girl stood in the door-way. The mountaineer was coming back from work with his face down.

"He hain't seed her yit," said one. "He's goin' to kill her shore. I tol'

her he would. She said she reckoned
he would, but she didn't keer."

For a moment I was paralyzed by
the tragedy at hand. She was in the
door looking at him when he raised
his head. For one moment he stood
still, staring, and then he started towards her with a quickened step. I
started too, then, every step a torture,
and as I limped ahead she made a
gesture of terror and backed into the
room before him. The door closed,
and I listened for a pistol-shot and a
scream. It must have been done with
a knife, I thought, and quietly, for
when I was within ten paces of the
cabin he opened the door again. His
face was very white ; he held one hand
behind him, and he was nervously
fumbling at his chin with the other.

16

As he stepped towards me I caught the handle of a pistol in my side pocket and waited. He looked at me sharply.

" Did you say the preacher lived up thar?" he asked.

"Yes," I said, breathlessly.

In the door-way just then stood the girl with a bonnet in her hand, and at a nod from him they started up the hill towards the cottage. They came down again after a while, he stalking ahead, and she, after the mountain fashion, behind. And after this fashion I saw them at sunset next day pass over the bridge and into the mouth of the Gap whence they came. Through this Gap come strange people and strange tales from the Kentucky hills. Over it, sometimes, is the span of a rainbow.

A TRICK O' TRADE

A TRICK O' TRADE

STRANGER, I'm a separ*ate* man, an' I don't in*qui*site into no man's business; but you ax me straight, an' I tell ye straight: You watch ole Tom!

Now, I'll take ole Tom Perkins' word agin anybody's 'ceptin' when hit comes to a hoss trade ur a piece o' land. Fer in the tricks o' sech, ole Tom 'lows— well, hit's diff'ent; an' I reckon, stranger, as how hit sorter is. He was a-stayin' at Tom's house, the furriner was, a-dickerin' fer a piece o' lan'—the same piece, mebbe, that you're atter now—

an' Tom keeps him thar fer a week to
beat him out'n a dollar, an' then won't
let him pay nary a cent fer his boa'd.
Now, stranger, that's Tom.

Well, Abe Shivers was a-workin' fer
Tom — you've heerd tell o' Abe — an'
the furriner wasn't more'n half gone
afore Tom seed that Abe was up to
some of his devil*mint*. Abe kin hatch
up more devil*mint* in a minit than Satan
hisself kin in a week; so Tom jes got
Abe out'n the stable under a hoe-handle,
an' tol' him to tell the whole thing
straight ur he'd have to go to glory
right thar. An' Abe tol'!

'Pears like Abe had foun' a streak o'
iron ore on the lan', an' had racked his
jinny right down to Hazlan an' tol' the
furriner, who was thar a-buyin' wild
lands right an' left. Co'se, Abe was

goin' to make the furriner whack up fer gittin' the lan' so cheap. Well, brother, the furriner come up to Tom's an' got Tom into one o' them new-fangled trades whut the furriners calls a option—t'other feller kin git out'n hit, but you can't. The furriner 'lowed he'd send his podner up thar next day to put the thing in writin' an' close up the trade. Hit looked like ole Tom was ketched fer shore, an' ef Tom didn't ra'r, I'd tell a man. He jes let that hoe-handle drap on Abe fer 'bout haffen hour, jes to give him time to study, an' next day thar was ole Tom a-settin' on his orchard fence a-lookin' mighty unknowin', when the furriner's podner come a-prancin' up an' axed ef old Tom Perkins lived thar.

Ole Tom jes whispers.

23

Now, I clean fergot to tell ye, stranger, that Abe Shivers nuver could talk out loud. He tol' so many lies that the Lawd—jes to make things even—sorter fixed Abe, I reckon, so he couldn't lie on 'more'n one side o' the river at a time. Ole Tom jes knowed t'other furriner had tol' this un 'bout Abe, an,' shore 'nough, the feller says, sorter soft, says he:

"Aw, you air the feller whut foun' the ore?"

Ole Tom — makin' like he was Abe, mind ye—jes whispers: "Thar hain't none thar."

Stranger, the feller mos' fell off'n his hoss. "Whut?" says he. Ole Tom kep' a-whisperin': "Thar hain't no coal— no nothing; ole Tom Perkins made me tell t'other furriner them lies."

Well, sir, the feller *was* mad. "Jes whut I tol' that fool podner of mine," he says, an' he pull out a dollar an' gives hit to Tom. Tom jes sticks out his han' with his thum' turned in jes so, an' the furriner says, "Well, ef you can't talk, you kin make purty damn good signs"; but he forks over four mo' dollars (he 'lowed ole Tom had saved him a pile o' money), an' turns his hoss an' pulls up agin. He was a-gittin' the land so durned cheap that I reckon he jes hated to let hit go, an' he says, says he: "Well, hain't the groun' rich? Won't hit raise no tabaccy nur corn nur nothin'?"

Ole Tom jes whispers:

"To tell you the p'int-blank truth, stranger, that land's so durned pore that I hain't nuver been able to raise my voice."

Now, brother, I'm a separate man, an' I don't inquizite into no man's business—but you ax me straight an' I tell ye straight. Ole Tom Perkins kin trade with furriners, fer he have l'arned their ways. You watch ole Tom!

GRAYSON'S BABY

THE first snow sifted in through the Gap that night, and in a "shack" of one room and a low loft a man was dead, a woman was sick to death, and four children were barely alive; and nobody even knew. For they were hill people, who sicken, suffer, and sometimes die, like animals, and make no noise.

Grayson, the Virginian, coming down from the woods that morning, saw the big-hearted little doctor outside the door of the shack, walking up and down, with his hands in his pockets. He was whistling softly when Grayson got near, and, without stopping, pointed with his thumb within. The oldest boy sat stolidly on the one chair in the room, his little brother was on the floor hard by, and both were hugging a greasy stove. The little girl was with her mother in the bed, both almost out of sight under a heap of quilts. The baby was in a cradle, with its face uncovered, whether dead or asleep Grayson could not tell. A pine coffin was behind the door. It would not have been possible to add to the disorder of the room, and the atmosphere made Grayson gasp. He came out looking white. The first man to arrive thereafter took away the eldest boy, a woman picked the baby girl from the bed, and a childless young couple took up the pallid little fellow on the floor. These were step-children. The baby-boy that was left was the woman's own. Nobody came for that, and Grayson went in again and looked at it a long while. So little, so old a human face he had never seen. The brow was wrinkled as with centuries of pain, and the little drawn mouth looked as though the spirit within had fought its inheritance without a murmur, and would fight on that way to the end. It was the pluck of the face that drew Grayson. "I'll take it," he said. The doctor was not without his sense of humor even then, but he nodded. "Cradle and all," he said, gravely. And Grayson put both on one shoulder and walked away. He had lost the power of giving further surprise in that town, and had he met

every man he knew, not one of them
would have felt at liberty to ask him
what he was doing. An hour later the
doctor found the child in Grayson's
room, and Grayson still looking at it.

"Is it going to live, doctor?"

The doctor shook his head. "Doubt-
ful. Look at the color. It's starved.
There's nothing to do but to watch it
and feed it. You can do that."

So Grayson watched it, with a fas-
cination of which he was hardly con-
scious. Never for one instant did its
look change—the quiet, unyielding en-
durance that no faith and no philosophy
could ever bring to him. It was ideal
courage, that look, to accept the inevit-
able but to fight it just that way. Half
the little mountain town was talking
next day—that such a tragedy was pos-

sible by the public road-side, with relief within sound of the baby's cry. The oldest boy was least starved. Might made right in an extremity like his, and the boy had taken care of himself. The young couple who had the second lad in charge said they had been wakened at daylight the next morning by some noise in the room. Looking up, they saw the little fellow at the fireplace breaking an egg. He had built a fire, had got eggs from the kitchen, and was cooking his breakfast. The little girl was mischievous and cheery in spite of her bad plight, and nobody knew of the baby except Grayson and the doctor. Grayson would let nobody else in. As soon as it was well enough to be peevish and to cry, he took it back to its mother, who was still abed. A long, dark moun-

taineer was there, of whom the woman
seemed half afraid.   He followed Grayson outside.

"Say, podner," he said, with an un-
pleasant smile, "ye don't go up to
Cracker's Neck fer nothin', do ye?"

The woman had lived at Cracker's
Neck before she appeared at the Gap,
and it did not come to Grayson what
the man meant until he was half-way to
his room.   Then he flushed hot and
wheeled back to the cabin, but the
mountaineer was gone.

"Tell that fellow he had better keep
out of my way," he said to the woman, who understood, and wanted to say
something, but not knowing how, nodded
simply.   In a few days the other children went back to the cabin, and day
and night Grayson went to see the child,

until it was out of danger, and afterwards. It was not long before the women
in town complained that the mother was
ungrateful. When they sent things to
eat to her the servant brought back
word that she had called out, "'Set
them over thar,' without so much as a
thanky." One message was that "she
didn' want no second-hand victuals from
nobody's table." Somebody suggested
sending the family to the poor-house.
The mother said "she'd go out on her
crutches and hoe corn fust, and that the
people who talked 'bout sendin' her to
the po'-house had better save their breath
to make prayers with." One day she
was hired to do some washing. The
mistress of the house happened not to
rise until ten o'clock. Next morning
the mountain woman did not appear

until that hour. "She wasn't goin' to work a lick while that woman was a-layin' in bed," she said, frankly. And when the lady went down town, she too disappeared. Nor would she, she explained to Grayson, " while that woman was a-struttin' the streets."

After that, one by one, they let her alone, and the woman made not a word of complaint. Within a week she was working in the fields, when she should have been back in bed. The result was that the child sickened again. The old look came back to its face, and Grayson was there night and day. He was having trouble out in Kentucky about this time, and he went to the Blue Grass pretty often. Always, however, he left money with me to see that the child was properly buried if it should die while he was gone; and once he telegraphed to ask how it was. He said he was sometimes afraid to open my letters for fear that he should read that the baby was dead. The child knew Grayson's voice, his step. It would go to him from its own mother. When it was sickest and lying torpid it would move the instant he stepped into the room, and, when he spoke, would hold out its thin arms, without opening its eyes, and for hours Grayson would walk the floor with the troubled little baby over his shoulder. I thought several times it would die when, on one trip, Grayson was away for two weeks. One midnight, indeed, I found the mother moaning, and three female harpies about the cradle. The baby was dying this time, and I ran back for a flask of whiskey. Ten minutes late with the whiskey that night would have been too late. The baby got to know me and my voice during that fortnight, but it was still in danger when Grayson got back, and we went to see it together. It was very weak, and we both leaned over the cradle, from either side, and I saw the pity and affection—yes, hungry, half-shamed affection — in Grayson's face. The child opened its eyes, looked from one to the other, and held out its arms to *me*. Grayson should have known that the child forgot—that it would forget its own mother. He turned sharply, and his face was a little pale. He gave something to the woman, and not till then did I notice

38

that her soft black eyes never left him while he was in the cabin. The child got well; but Grayson never went to the shack again, and he said nothing when I came in one night and told him that some mountaineer —a long, dark fellow—had taken the woman, the children, and the household gods of the shack back into the mountains.

"They don't grieve long," I said, "these people."

But long afterwards I saw the woman again along the dusty road that leads into the Gap. She had heard over in the mountains that Grayson was dead, and had walked for two days to learn if it was true. I pointed back towards Bee Rock, and told her that he had fallen from a cliff back there. She did not move, nor did her look change. Moreover, she said nothing, and, being in a hurry, I had to ride on.

At the foot-bridge over Roaring Fork I looked back. The woman was still there, under the hot mid-day sun and in the dust of the road, motionless.

COURTIN' ON CUTSHIN

HIT was this way, stranger. When hit comes to handlin' a right peert gal, Jeb Somers air about the porest man on Fryin' Pan, I reckon ; an' Polly Ann Sturgill have got the vineg'rest tongue on Cutshin or any other crick.

So the boys over on Fryin' Pan made it up to git 'em together. Abe Shivers — you've heerd tell o' Abe — tol' Jeb that Polly Ann had seed him in Hazlan (which she hadn't, of co'se), an' had said p'int-blank that he was the likeliest feller she'd seed in them

43

mountains. An' he tol' Polly Ann
that Jeb was ravin' crazy 'bout her.
The pure misery of it jes made him
plumb delirious, Abe said; an' 'f Polly
Ann wanted to find her match fer lan-
guige an' talkin' out peert — well, she
jes ought to strike Jeb Somers. Fact
is, stranger, Jeb Somers air might' nigh
a idgit; but Jeb 'lowed he'd rack right
over on Cutshin an' set up with Polly
Ann Sturgill; an' Abe tells Polly Ann
the king bee air comin'. An' Polly
Ann's cousin, Nance Osborn, comes
over from Hell fer Sartain (whut runs
into Kingdom-Come) to stay all night
an' see the fun.

Now, I hain't been a-raftin' logs
down to the settlemints o' Kaintuck
fer nigh on to twenty year fer nothin'. An' I know gallivantin' is diff'ent

with us mountain fellers an' you furriners, in the premises, anyways, as
them lawyers up to court says; though
I reckon hit's purty much the same
atter the premises is over. Whar you
says "courtin'," now, we says "talkin'
to." Sallie Spurlock over on Fryin'
Pan is a-talkin' to Jim Howard now.
Sallie's sister hain't nuver talked to no
man. An' whar you says "makin' a
call on a young lady," we says "settin'
up with a gal"! An', stranger, we does
it. We hain't got more'n one room
hardly ever in these mountains, an'
we're jes obleeged to set up to do any
courtin' at all.

Well, you go over to Sallie's to stay
all night some time, an' purty soon
atter supper Jim Howard comes in.
The ole man an' the ole woman goes

to bed, an' the chil'un an' you go to bed, an' ef you keeps one eye open you'll see Jim's cheer an' Sallie's cheer a-movin' purty soon, till they gets plumb together. Then, stranger, hit begins. Now I want ye to understand that settin' up means business. We don't 'low no foolishness in these mountains; an' 'f two fellers happens to meet at the same house, they jes makes the gal say which one she likes best, an' t'other one gits! Well, you'll see Jim put his arm 'round Sallie's neck an' whisper a long while—jes so. Mebbe you've noticed whut fellers us mountain folks air fer whisperin'. You've seed fellers a-whisperin' all over Hazlan on court day, hain't ye? Ole Tom Perkins 'll put his arm aroun' yo' neck an' whisper in yo' year ef he's ten mile out'n the woods. I reckon thar's jes so much devilmint a-goin' on in these mountains, folks is naturely afeerd to talk out loud.

Well, Jim let's go an' Sallie puts her arm aroun' Jim's neck an' whispers a long while — jes so; an' 'f you happen to wake up anywhar to two o'clock in the mornin' you'll see jes that a-goin' on. Brother, that's settin' up.

Well, Jeb Somers, as I was a-sayin' in the premises, 'lowed he'd rack right over on Cutshin an' set up with Polly Ann comin' Christmas night. An' Abe tells Polly Ann Jeb says he aims to have her fer a Christmas gift afore mornin'. Polly Ann jes sniffed sorter, but you know women folks air always mighty ambitious jes to *see* a feller anyways, 'f he's a-pinin' fer 'em. So

Jeb come, an' Jeb was fixed up now fittin' to kill. Jeb had his hair oiled down nice an' slick, and his mustache was jes black as powder could make hit. Naturely hit was red; but a feller can't do nothin' in these mountains with a red mustache; an' Jeb had a big black ribbon tied in the butt o' the bigges' pistol Abe Shivers could borrer fer him—hit was a badge o' death an' deestruction to his enemies, Abe said, an' I tell ye Jeb did look like a man. He never opened his mouth atter he says "howdy"—Jeb never does say nothin'; Jeb's one o' them fellers whut hides thar lack o' brains by a-lookin' solemn an' a-keepin' still, but thar don't nobody say much tell the ole folks air gone to bed, an' Polly Ann jes 'lowed Jeb was a-waitin'.

48

Fact is, stranger, Abe Shivers had got
Jeb a leetle disguised by liquer, an' he
did look fat an' sassy, ef he couldn't
talk, a-settin' over in the corner a-
plunkin' the banjer an' a-knockin' off
" Sour-wood Mountain " an' " Jinny git
aroun' " an' "Soapsuds over the Fence."

" Chickens a-crowin' on Sour-wood Mountain,
    Heh-o-dee-um-dee-eedy-dahdy-dee!
  Git yo' dawgs an' we'll go huntin',
    Heh-o-dee-um-dee-eedy-dahdy-dee !"

An' when Jeb comes to

" I've got a gal at the head o' the holler,
    Heh-o-dee-um-dee-eedy-dahdy-dee !"

he jes turns one eye 'round on Polly
Ann, an' then swings his chin aroun' as
though he didn't give a cuss fer nothin'.

"She won't come, an' I won't foller,
    Heh-o-dee-um-dee-eedy-dahdy-dee !"

Well, sir, Nance seed that Polly Ann
was a-eyin' Jeb sort o' flustered like,
an' she come might' nigh splittin' right
thar an' a-sp'ilin' the fun, fer she
knowed what a skeery fool Jeb was.
An' when the ole folks goes to bed,
Nance lays thar under a quilt a-watchin' an' a-listenin'. Well, Jeb knowed
the premises, ef he couldn't talk, an'
purty soon Nance heerd Jeb's cheer
creak a leetle, an' she says, Jeb's a-
comin', and Jeb was; an' Polly Ann
'lowed Jeb was jes a leetle *too* resolute
an' quick-like, an' she got her hand
ready to give him one lick anyways
fer bein' so brigaty. I don't know as
she'd 'a' hit him more'n *once*. Jeb had
a farm, an' Polly Ann—well, Polly Ann
was a-gittin' along. But Polly Ann
sot thar jes as though she didn't know

Jeb was a-comin', an' Jeb stopped once an' says,

"You hain't got nothin' agin me, has ye?"

An' Polly Ann says, sorter quick,

"Naw; ef I had, I'd push it."

Well, Jeb mos' fell off his cheer, when, ef he hadn't been sech a skeery idgit, he'd 'a' knowed that Polly Ann was plain open an' shet a-biddin' fer him. But he sot thar like a knot on a log fer haffen hour, an' then he rickollected, I reckon, that Abe had tol' him Polly Ann was peppery an' he mustn't mind, fer Jeb begun a-movin' ag'in till he was slam-bang agin Polly Ann's cheer. An' thar he sot like a punkin, not sayin' a word nur doin' nothin'. An' while Polly Ann was a-wonderin' ef he was gone plumb crazy, blame me ef that durned

fool didn't turn roun' to that peppery
gal an' say,

"Booh, Polly Ann!"

Well, Nance had to stuff the bedquilt
in her mouth right thar to keep from
hollerin' out loud, fer Polly Ann's hand
was a-hangin' down by the cheer, jes
a-waitin' fer a job, and Nance seed the
fingers a-twitchin'. An' Jeb waits another haffen hour an' Jeb says,

"Ortern't I be killed?"

"Whut fer?" says Polly Ann, sorter
sharp.

An' Jeb says, "Fer bein' so devilish."

Well, brother, Nance snorted right
out thar, an' Polly Ann Sturgill's hand
riz up jes once; an' I've heerd Jeb
Somers say the next time he jumps out
o' the Fryin' Pan he's a-goin' to take hell-
fire 'stid o' Cutshin fer a place to light.

THE MESSAGE IN THE SAND

THE MESSAGE IN THE SAND

STRANGER, you furriners don't nuver seem to consider that a woman has always got the devil to fight in two people at once! Hit's two agin one, I tell ye, an' hit hain't fa'r.

That's what I said more'n two year ago, when Rosie Branham was a-layin' up thar at Dave Hall's, white an' mos' dead. An', *God*, boys, I says, that leetle thing in thar by her shorely can't be to blame.

Thar hain't been a word agin Rosie sence; an', stranger, I reckon thar nuver will be. Fer, while the gal hain't got hide o' kith or kin, thar air two fellers up hyeh sorter lookin' atter Rosie; an' one of 'em is the shootin'es' man on this crick, I reckon, 'cept one; an', stranger, that's t'other.

Rosie kep' her mouth shet fer a long while; an' I reckon as how the feller 'lowed she wasn't goin' to tell. Co'se the woman folks got hit out'n her—they al'ays gits whut they want, as you know —an' thar the sorry cuss was—a-livin' up thar in the Bend, jes aroun' that bluff o' lorrel yander, a-lookin' pious, an' a-singin', an' a-sayin' Amen louder 'n anybody when thar was meetin'.

Well, my boy Jim an' a lot o' fellers jes went up fer him right away. I don't know as the boys would 'a' killed him *exactly* ef they had kotched him, though they mought; but they got Abe Shivers, as tol' the feller they was a-comin'— you've heard tell o' Abe—an' they mos' beat Abraham Shivers to death. Stranger, the sorry cuss was Dave. Rosie hadn't no daddy an' no mammy; an' she was jes a-workin' at Dave's fer her victuals an' clo'es. 'Pears like the pore gal was jes tricked into evil. Looked like she was sorter 'witched—an' anyways, stranger, she was a-fightin' Satan in *herself*, as well as in Dave. Hit was two agin one, I tell ye, an' hit wasn't fa'r.

Co'se they turned Rosie right out in the road. I hain't got a word to say agin Dave's wife fer that; an' atter a while the boys lets Dave come back, to take keer o' his ole mammy, of co'se, but I tell ye Dave's a-playin' a purty lonesome tune. He keeps purty shy *yit*. He don't nuver sa'nter down this way. 'Pears like he don't seem to think hit's healthy fer him down hyeh, an' I reckon Dave's right.

Rosie? Oh, well, I sorter tuk Rosie in myself. Yes, she's been livin' thar in the shack with me an' my boy Jim, an' the— Why, thar he is now, stranger. That's him a-wallerin' out thar in the road. Do you reckon thar'd be a single thing agin that leetle cuss ef he had to stan' up on Jedgment Day jes as he is now?

Look hyeh, stranger, whut you reckon the Lawd kep' a-writin' thar on the groun' that day when them fellers was a-pesterin' him 'bout that pore woman? Don't you jes know he was a writin' 'bout sech as *him*— an' Rosie? I tell

58

ye, brother, he writ thar jes what I'm al'ays a-sayin'.

Hit hain't the woman's fault. I said it more'n two year ago, when Rosie was up thar at ole Dave's, an' I said it yestiddy, when my boy Jim come to me an' 'lowed as how he aimed to take Rosie down to town to-day an' git married.

"You ricollect, dad," says Jim, "her mammy?"

"Yes, Jim," I says; "all the better reason not to be too hard on Rosie."

I'm a-lookin' fer 'em both back right now, stranger; an' ef you will, I'll be mighty glad to have ye stay right hyeh to the infair this very night. Thar nuver was a word agin Rosie afore, thar hain't been sence, an' you kin ride up an' down this river till the crack o' doom an' you'll nuver hear a word agin her ag'in. Fer, as I tol' you, my boy, Jim is the shootin'es' feller on this crick, I reckon, 'cept *one*, an', stranger, that's *me !*

THE SENATOR'S LAST TRADE

A DROVE of lean cattle were swinging easily over Black Mountain, and behind them came a big man with wild black hair and a bushy beard. Now and then he would gnaw at his mustache with his long, yellow teeth, or would sit down to let his lean horse rest, and would flip meaninglessly at the bushes with a switch. Sometimes his bushy head would droop over on his breast, and he would snap it up sharply and start painfully on. Robber, cattle-thief, outlaw he might have

been in another century; for he filled
the figure of any robber hero in life
or romance, and yet he was only the
Senator from Bell, as he was known
in the little Kentucky capital; or, as
he was known in his mountain home,
just the Senator, who had toiled and
schemed and grown rich and grown poor;
who had suffered long and was kind.

Only that Christmas he had gutted
every store in town. "Give me everything you have, brother," he said, across
each counter; and next day every man,
woman, and child in the mountain
town had a present from the Senator's
hands. He looked like a brigand that
day, as he looked now, but he called
every man his brother, and his eye,
while black and lustreless as night, was
as brooding and just as kind.

When the boom went down, with it
and with everybody else went the Senator. Slowly he got dusty, ragged,
long of hair. He looked tortured and
ever-restless. You never saw him still;
always he swept by you, flapping his
legs on his lean horse or his arms in
his rickety buggy here, there, everywhere—turning, twisting, fighting his
way back to freedom—and not a murmur. Still was every man his brother,
and if some forgot his once open hand,
he forgot it no more completely than
did the Senator. He went very far to
pay his debts. He felt honor bound,
indeed, to ask his sister to give back
the farm that he had given her, which,
very properly people said, she declined
to do. Nothing could kill hope in the
Senator's breast; he would hand back

the farm in another year, he said; but
the sister was firm, and without a word
still, the Senator went other ways and
schemed through the nights, and worked and rode and walked and traded
through the days, until now, when the
light was beginning to glimmer, his
end was come.

This was the Senator's last trade, and
in sight, down in a Kentucky valley,
was home. Strangely enough, the Senator did not care at all, and he had
just enough sanity left to wonder why,
and to be worried. It was the "walking typhoid" that had caught up with
him, and he was listless, and he made
strange gestures and did foolish things
as he stumbled down the mountain.
He was going over a little knoll now,
and he could see the creek that ran

around his house, but he was not touched. He would just as soon have lain down right where he was, or have turned around and gone back, except that it was hot and he wanted to get to the water. He remembered that it was nigh Christmas; he saw the snow about him and the cakes of ice in the creek. He knew that he ought not to be hot, and yet he was—so hot that he refused to reason with himself even a minute, and hurried on. It was odd that it should be so, but just about that time, over in Virginia, a cattle-dealer, nearing home, stopped to tell a neighbor how he had tricked some black-whiskered fool up in the mountains. It may have been just when he was laughing aloud over there, that the Senator, over here, tore his woollen shirt from his great hairy chest and rushed into the icy stream, clapping his arms to his burning sides and shouting in his frenzy.

" If he had lived a little longer," said a constituent, " he would have lost the next election. He hadn't the money, you know."

" If he had lived a little longer," said the mountain preacher high up on Yellow Creek, " I'd have got that trade I had on hand with him through. Not that I wanted him to die, but if he had to—why—"

" If he had lived a little longer," said the Senator's lawyer, " he would have cleaned off the score against him."

" If he had lived a little longer," said the Senator's sister, not meaning to

68

be unkind, "he would have got all I have."

That was what life held for the Senator. Death was more kind.

PREACHIN' ON KINGDOM-COME

I'VE told ye, stranger, that Hell fer Sartain empties, as it oughter, of co'se, into Kingdom-Come. You can ketch the devil 'most any day in the week on Hell fer Sartain, an' sometimes you can git Glory everlastin' on Kingdom-Come. Hit's the only meetin'-house thar in twenty miles aroun'.

Well, the reg'lar rider, ole Jim Skaggs, was dead, an' the bretherin was a-lookin' aroun' fer somebody to step into ole Jim's shoes. Thar'd been one young feller up thar from the settlemints, a-cavortin' aroun', an' they was studyin' 'bout gittin' him.

"Bretherin' an' sisteren," I says, atter the leetle chap was gone, "he's got the fortitood to speak an' he shorely is well favored. He's got a mighty good hawk eye fer spyin' out evil—an' the gals; he can outholler ole Jim; an' *if*," I says, "any *idees* ever comes to him, he'll be a hell-rouser shore—but they ain't comin'!" An', so sayin', I takes my foot in my hand an' steps fer home.

Stranger, them fellers over thar hain't seed much o' this world. Lots of 'em nuver seed the cyars; some of 'em nuver seed a wagon. An' atter jowerin' an' noratin' fer 'bout two hours, what you reckon they said they aimed to do? They believed they'd take that ar man Beecher, ef they could git him to come.

They'd heerd o' Henry endurin' the war, an' they knowed he was agin the rebs, an' they wanted Henry if they could jes git him to come.

Well, I snorted, an' the feud broke out on Hell fer Sartain betwixt the Days an' the Dillons. Mace Day shot Daws Dillon's brother, as I rickollect—some-p'n's al'ays a-startin' up that plaguey war an' a-makin' things frolicsome over thar—an' ef it hadn't a-been fer a tall young feller with black hair an' a scar across his forehead, who was a-goin' through the mountains a-settlin' these wars, blame me ef I believe thar ever would 'a' been any mo' preachin' on Kingdom-Come. This feller comes over from Hazlan an' says he aims to hold a meetin' on Kingdom-Come. "Brother," I says, "that's what no preacher have

ever did whilst this war is a-goin' on."
An' he says, sort o' quiet, "Well, then, I
reckon I'll have to do what no preacher
have ever did." An' I ups an' says:
"Brother, an ole jedge come up here
once from the settlemints to hold couht.
'Jedge,' I says, 'that's what no jedge
have ever did without soldiers since this
war's been a-goin' on.' An', brother, the
jedge's words was yours, p'int-blank.
'All right,' he says, 'then I'll have to do
what no other jedge have ever did.'
An', brother," says I to the preacher,
"the jedge done it shore. He jes laid
under the couht-house fer two days whilst
the boys fit over him. An' when I sees
the jedge a-makin' tracks fer the settlemints, I says, ' Jedge,' I says, ' you spoke
a parable shore.' "

Well, sir, the long preacher looked

jes as though he was a-sayin' to hisself,
" Yes, I hear ye, but I don't heed ye,"
an' when he says, " Jes the same, I'm
a-goin' to hold a meetin' on Kingdom-
Come," why, I jes takes my foot in my
hand an' ag'in I steps fer home.

That night, stranger, I seed another
feller from Hazlan, who was a-tellin' how
this here preacher had stopped the war
over thar, an' had got the Marcums an'
Braytons to shakin' hands; an' next day
ole Tom Perkins stops in an' says that
wharas there mought 'a' been preachin'
somewhar an' sometime, thar nuver had
been *preachin'* afore on Kingdom-Come.
So I goes over to the meetin'-house, an'
they was all thar — Daws Dillon an'
Mace Day, the leaders in the war, an'
Abe Shivers (you've heerd tell o' Abe)
who was a-carryin' tales from one side to

t'other an' a-stirrin' up hell ginerally, as
Abe most al'ays is; an' thar was Daws
on one side o' the meetin'-house an'
Mace on t'other, an' both jes a-watchin'
fer t'other to make a move, an' thar'd
'a' been billy-hell to pay right thar!
Stranger, that long preacher talked jes
as easy as I'm a-talkin' now, an' hit was
p'int-blank as the feller from Hazlan
said. You jes ought 'a' heerd him tellin'
about the Lawd a-bein' as pore as any
feller thar, an' a-makin' barns an' fences
an' ox-yokes an' sech like; an' not
a-bein' able to write his own name—
havin' to make his mark mebbe—when
he started out to save the world. An'
how they tuk him an' nailed him onto
a cross when he'd come down fer nothin'
but to save 'em; an' stuck a spear big as
a corn-knife into his side, an' give him

vinegar; an' his own mammy a-standin' down thar on the ground a-cryin' an' a-watchin' him; an' he a-fergivin' all of 'em then an' thar!

Thar nuver had been nothin' like that afore on Kingdom-Come, an' all along I heerd fellers a-layin' thar guns down; an' when the preacher called out fer sinners, blame me ef the fust feller that riz wasn't Mace Day. An' Mace says, "Stranger, 'f what you say is true, I reckon the Lawd 'll fergive me too, but I don't believe Daws Dillon ever will," an' Mace stood thar lookin' around fer Daws. An' all of a sudden the preacher got up straight an' called out, "Is thar a human in this house mean an' sorry enough to stand betwixt a man an' his Maker"? An' right thar, stranger, Daws riz. "Naw, by God, thar hain't!" Daws says, an' he walks up to Mace a-holdin' out his hand, an' they all busts out cryin' an' shakin' hands—Days an' Dillons—jes as the preacher had made 'em do over in Hazlan. An' atter the thing was over, I steps up to the preacher an' I says:

"Brother," I says, "*you* spoke a parable, shore."

THE PASSING OF ABRAHAM
SHIVERS

"I TELL ye, boys, hit hain't often a feller has the chance o' doin' so much good jes by *dyin'*. Fer 'f Abe Shivers air gone, shorely gone, the rest of us—every durn one of us—air a-goin' to be saved. Fer Abe Shivers — you hain't heerd tell o' *Abe ?* Well, you must be a stranger in these mountains o' Kaintuck, shore.

"I don't know, stranger, as Abe ever was borned; nobody in these mountains knows it 'f he was. The fust time I ever

heerd tell o' Abe he was a-hollerin' fer his
rights one mawnin' at daylight, endurin'
the war, jes outside o' ole Tom Perkins'
door on Fryin' Pan. Abe was left thar
by some home-gyard, I reckon. Well,
nobody air ever turned out'n doors in
these mountains, as you know, an' Abe
got his rights that mawin', an' he's been
a-gittin' 'em ever sence. Tom already
had a houseful, but 'f any feller got the
bigges' hunk o' corn-bread, that feller was
Abe; an' ef any feller got a-whalin',
hit wasn't Abe.

"Abe tuk to lyin' right naturely—
looked like—afore he could talk. Fact
is, Abe nuver could do nothin' but jes
whisper. Still, Abe could manage to
send a lie furder with that rattlin'
whisper than ole Tom could with
that big horn o' hisn what tells the

boys the revenoos air comin' up Fryin'
Pan.'

"Didn't take Abe long to git to brag-
gin' an' drinkin' an' naggin' an' hectorin'
—everything, 'mos', 'cept fightin'. Nobody ever drawed Abe Shivers into a
fight. I don't know as he was afeerd;
looked like Abe was a-havin' sech a tar-
nation good time with his devilmint he
jes didn't want to run no risk o' havin'
hit stopped. An' sech devilmint! Hit
ud take a coon's age, I reckon, to tell
ye.

"The boys was a-goin' up the river
one night to git ole Dave Hall fer trickin'
Rosie Branham into evil. Some feller
goes ahead an' tells ole Dave they's
a-comin.' Hit was Abe. Some feller
finds a streak o' ore on ole Tom Perkins'
land, an' racks his jinny down to town,

an' tells a furriner thar, an' Tom comes might' nigh sellin' the land fer nothin'. Now Tom raised Abe, but, jes the same, the feller was Abe.

"One night somebody guides the revenoos in on Hell fer Sartain, an' they cuts up four stills. Hit was Abe. The same night, mind ye, a feller slips in among the revenoos while they's asleep, and cuts off their hosses' manes an' tails — muled every durned critter uv 'em. Stranger, hit was Abe. An' as fer women-folks — well, Abe was the ill-favoredest feller I ever see, an' he couldn't talk; still, Abe was sassy, an' you know how sass counts with the gals; an' Abe's whisperin' come in jes as handy as any feller's settin' up; so 'f ever you seed a man with a Winchester a-lookin' fer the feller who had cut

him out, stranger, he was a-lookin' fer
Abe.

"Somebody tells Harve Hall, up thar
at a dance on Hell-fer-Sartain one Christmas night, that Rich Harp had said
somep'n' agin him an' Nance Osborn.
An' somebody tells Rich that Harve had
said sompe'n' agin Nance an' *him*.   Hit
was one an' the same feller, stranger, an'
the feller was Abe.   Well, while Rich
an' Harve was a-gittin' well, somebody
runs off with Nance.   Hit was Abe.
Then Rich an' Harve jes draws straws
fer a feller.   Stranger, they drawed fer
Abe.   Hit's purty hard to believe that
Abe air gone, 'cept that Rich Harp an'
Harve Hall don't never draw no straws
fer nothin'; but 'f by the grace o' Goddle-
mighty Abe air gone, why, as I was
a-sayin', the rest of us—every durned one

87

of us—air a-goin' to be saved, shore. Fer Abe's gone fust, an' ef thar's only one Jedgment Day, the Lawd 'll nuver git to us."

A PURPLE RHODODENDRON

A PURPLE RHODODENDRON

———

THE purple rhododendron is rare. Up in the Gap here, Bee Rock, hung out over Roaring Rock, blossoms with it—as a gray cloud purples with the sunrise. This rock was tossed lightly on edge when the earth was young, and stands vertical. To get the flowers you climb the mountain to one side, and, balancing on the rock's thin edge, slip down by roots and past rattlesnake dens till you hang out over the water and reach for them. To avoid snakes it is best to go when it is cool, at daybreak.

A PURPLE RHODODENDRON

I know but one other place in this southwest corner of Virginia where there is another bush of purple rhododendron, and one bush only is there. This hangs at the throat of a peak not far away, whose ageless gray head is bent over a ravine that sinks like a spear thrust into the side of the mountain. Swept only by high wind and eagle wings as this is, I yet knew one man foolhardy enough to climb to it for a flower. He brought one blossom down: and to this day I do not know that it was not the act of a coward; yes, though Grayson did it, actually smiling all the way from peak to ravine, and though he was my best friend —best loved then and since. I believe he was the strangest man I have ever known, and I say this with thought;

for his eccentricities were sincere. In all he did I cannot remember having even suspected anything theatrical but once.

We were all Virginians or Kentuckians at the Gap, and Grayson was a Virginian. You might have guessed that he was a Southerner from his voice and from the way he spoke of women —but no more. Otherwise, he might have been a Moor, except for his color, which was about the only racial characteristic he had. He had been educated abroad and, after the English habit, had travelled everywhere. And yet I can imagine no more lonely way between the eternities than the path Grayson trod alone.

He came to the Gap in the early days, and just why he came I never

knew. He had studied the iron question a long time, he told me, and what
I thought reckless speculation was, it
seems, deliberate judgment to him. His
money " in the dirt," as the phrase was,
Grayson got him a horse and rode the
hills and waited. He was intimate with
nobody. Occasionally he would play
poker with us and sometimes he drank
a good deal, but liquor never loosed his
tongue. At poker his face told as little
as the back of his cards, and he won more
than admiration — even from the Kentuckians, who are artists at the game ;
but the money went from a free hand,
and, after a diversion like this, he was
apt to be moody and to keep more to
himself than ever. Every fortnight or
two he would disappear, always over
Sunday. In three or four days he

would turn up again, black with brooding, and then he was the last man to
leave the card-table or he kept away
from it altogether. Where he went nobody knew; and he was not the man
anybody would question.

One night two of us Kentuckians
were sitting in the club, and from a
home paper I read aloud the rumored
engagement of a girl we both knew—
who was famous for beauty in the Bluegrass, as was her mother before her and
the mother before her—to an unnamed
Virginian. Grayson sat near, smoking a
pipe; and when I read the girl's name
I saw him take the meerschaum from
his lips, and I felt his eyes on me. It
was a mystery how, but I knew at once
that Grayson was the man. He sought
me out after that and seemed to want

to make friends. I was willing, or, rather he made me more than willing; for
he was irresistible to me, as I imagine
he would have been to anybody. We
got to walking together and riding together at night, and we were soon rather
intimate; but for a long time he never
so much as spoke the girl's name. Indeed, he kept away from the Bluegrass
for nearly two months; but when he
did go he stayed a fortnight.

This time he came for me as soon as
he got back to the Gap. It was just
before midnight, and we went as usual
back of Imboden Hill, through moon-
dappled beeches, and Grayson turned
off into the woods where there was
no path, both of us silent. We rode
through tremulous, shining leaves —
Grayson's horse choosing a way for him-

self — and, threshing through a patch
of high, strong weeds, we circled past an
amphitheatre of deadened trees whose
crooked arms were tossed out into the
moonlight, and halted on the spur. The
moon was poised over Morris's farm ;
South Fork was shining under us like a
loop of gold, the mountains lay about in
tranquil heaps, and the moon-mist rose
luminous between them. There Grayson turned to me with an eager light in
his eyes that I had never seen before.

"This has a new beauty to-night!"
he said; and then "I told her about
you, and she said that she used to know
you—well." I was glad my face was in
shadow — I could hardly keep back a
brutal laugh — and Grayson, unseeing,
went on to speak of her as I had never
heard any man speak of any woman. In

the end, he said that she had just prom-
ised to be his wife. I answered nothing. Other men, I knew, had said that
with the same right, perhaps, and had
gone from her to go back no more.
And I was one of them. Grayson had
met her at White Sulphur five years
before, and had loved her ever since.
She had known it from the first, he
said, and I guessed then what was going
to happen to him. I marvelled, listening to the man, for it was the star of
constancy in her white soul that was
most lustrous to him—and while I won-
dered the marvel became a common-
place. Did not every lover think his
loved one exempt from the frailty that
names other women? There is no ideal
of faith or of purity that does not live
in countless women to-day. I believe

that; but could I not recall one friend who walked with Divinity through pine woods for one immortal spring, and who, being sick to death, was quite finished —learning her at last? Did I not know lovers who believed sacred to them-selves, in the name of love, lips that had been given to many another with-out it? And now did I not know—but I knew too much, and to Grayson I said nothing.

That spring the "boom" came. Gray-son's property quadrupled in value and quadrupled again. I was his lawyer,,and I plead with him to sell; but Grayson laughed. He was not speculating; he had invested on judgment; he would sell only at a certain figure. The figure was actually reached, and Grayson let half go. The boom fell, and Grayson took the tumble with a jest. It would come again in the autumn, he said, and he went off to meet the girl at White Sulphur.

I worked right hard that summer, but I missed him, and I surely was glad when he came back. Something was wrong; I saw it at once. He did not mention her name, and for a while he avoided even me. I sought him then, and gradually I got him into our old habit of walking up into the Gap and of sitting out after supper on a big rock in the valley, listening to the run of the river and watching the afterglow over the Cumberland, the moon rise over Wallen's Ridge and the stars come out. Waiting for him to speak, I learned for the first time then another secret of his wretched melancholy. It was the hope-

lessness of that time, perhaps, that dis-
closed it.   Grayson had lost the faith
of his childhood.   Most men do that at
some time or other, but Grayson had
no business, no profession, no art in
which to find relief.   Indeed, there was
but one substitute possible, and that
came like a gift straight from the God
whom he denied. Love came, and Grayson's ideals of love, as of everything
else, were morbid and quixotic.   He
believed that he owed it to the woman
he should marry never to have loved
another.   He had loved but one woman, he said, and he should love but one.
I believed him then literally when he
said that his love for the Kentucky
girl was his religion now — the only
anchor left him in his sea of troubles,
the only star that gave him guid-

ing light. Without this love, what then?

I had a strong impulse to ask him, but Grayson shivered, as though he divined my thought, and, in some relentless way, our talk drifted to the question of suicide. I was not surprised that he rather defended it. Neither of us said anything new, only I did not like the way he talked. He was too deliberate, too serious, as though he were really facing a possible fact. He had no religious scruples, he said, no family ties; he had nothing to do with bringing himself into life; why — if it was not worth living, not bearable— why should he not end it? He gave the usual authority, and I gave the usual answer. Religion aside, if we did not know that we were here for some purpose, we did not know that we were not ; and here we were anyway, and our duty was plain. Desertion was the act of a coward, and that Grayson could not deny.

That autumn the crash of '91 came across the water from England, and Grayson gave up. He went to Richmond, and came back with money enough to pay off his notes, and I think it took nearly all he had. Still, he played poker steadily now—for poker had been resumed when it was no longer possible to gamble in lots—he drank a good deal, and he began just at this time to take a singular interest in our volunteer police guard. He had always been on hand when there was trouble, and I sha'n't soon forget him the day Senator Mahone spoke, when we were

punching a crowd of mountaineers back
with cocked Winchesters. He had lost
his hat in a struggle with one giant; he
looked half crazy with anger, and yet
he was white and perfectly cool, and I
noticed that he never had to tell a man
but once to stand back. Now he was
the first man to answer a police whistle.
When we were guarding Talt Hall, he
always volunteered when there was any
unusual risk to run. When we raided
the Pound to capture a gang of despe-
radoes, he insisted on going ahead as
spy; and when we got restless lying
out in the woods waiting for daybreak,
and the captain suggested a charge on
the cabin, Grayson was by his side when
it was made. Grayson sprang through
the door first, and he was the man who
thrust his reckless head up into the loft

and lighted a match to see if the murderers were there. Most of us did foolish things in those days under stress of excitement, but Grayson, I saw, was weak enough to be reckless. His trouble with the girl, whatever it was, was serious enough to make him apparently care little whether he were alive or dead. And still I saw that not yet even had he lost hope. He was having a sore fight with his pride, and he got bodyworn and heart-sick over it. Of course he was worsted, and in the end, from sheer weakness, he went back to her once more.

I shall never see another face like his when Grayson came back that last time. I never noticed before that there were silver hairs about his temples. He stayed in his room, and had his meals sent to

him. He came out only to ride, and then
at night. Waking the third morning at
daybreak, I saw him through the window
galloping past, and I knew he had spent
the night on Black Mountain. I went
to his room as soon as I got up, and
Grayson was lying across his bed with
his face down, his clothes on, and in his
right hand was a revolver. I reeled
into a chair before I had strength enough
to bend over him, and when I did I
found him asleep. I left him as he was,
and I never let him know that I had
been to his room ; but I got him out on
the rock again that night, and I turned
our talk again to suicide. I said it was
small, mean, cowardly, criminal, con-
temptible! I was savagely in earnest,
and Grayson shivered and said not a
word. I thought he was in better mind

after that. We got to taking night
rides again, and I stayed as closely to
him as I could, for times got worse and
trouble was upon everybody. Notes fell
thicker than snowflakes, and, through
the foolish policy of the company, fore-
closures had to be made. Grayson went
to the wall like the rest of us. I asked
him what he had done with the money
he had made. He had given away a
great deal to poorer kindred; he had
paid his dead father's debts; he had
played away a good deal, and he had
lost the rest. His faith was still imper-
turbable. He had a dozen rectangles of
" dirt," and from these, he said, it would
all come back some day. Still, he felt
the sudden poverty keenly, but he faced
it as he did any other physical fact in
life—dauntless. He used to be fond of

saying that no one thing could make
him miserable. But he would talk with
mocking earnestness about some much-
dreaded combination; and a favorite
phrase of his—which got to have peculiar
significance—was "the cohorts of hell,"
who closed in on him when he was sick
and weak, and who fell back when he
got well. He had one strange habit,
too, from which I got comfort. He
would deliberately walk into and defy
any temptation that beset him. That
was the way he strengthened himself,
he said. I knew what his temptation
was now, and I thought of this habit
when I found him asleep with his revolver, and I got hope from it now,
when the dreaded combination (whatever
that was) seemed actually to have come.

I could see now that he got worse

daily. He stopped his mockeries, his
occasional fits of reckless gayety. He
stopped poker—resolutely—he couldn't
afford to lose now; and, what puzzled me,
he stopped drinking. The man simply
looked tired, always hopelessly tired;
and I could believe him sincere in all
his foolish talk about his blessed Nir-
vana: which was the peace he craved,
which was end enough for him.

Winter broke. May drew near; and
one afternoon, when Grayson and I took
our walk up through the Gap, he carried
along a huge spy-glass of mine, which
had belonged to a famous old desperado,
who watched his enemies with it from the
mountain-tops. We both helped capture
him, and I defended him. He was sen-
tenced to hang—the glass was my fee.
We sat down opposite Bee Rock, and

for the first time Grayson told me of
that last scene with her. He spoke
without bitterness, and he told me what
she said, word for word, without a breath
of blame for her. I do not believe that
he judged her at all; she did not know—
he always said; she did not *know;* and
then, when I opened my lips, Grayson
reached silently for my wrist, and I can
feel again the warning crush of his fingers, and I say nothing against her now.

I asked Grayson what his answer was.

"I asked her," he said, solemnly, "if
she had ever seen a purple rhododendron."

I almost laughed, picturing the scene
—the girl bewildered by his absurd question—Grayson calm, superbly courteous.
It was a mental peculiarity of his—this
irrelevancy—and it was like him to end

a matter of life and death in just that way.

"I told her I should send her one. I am waiting for them to come out," he added; and he lay back with his head against a stone and sighted the telescope on a dizzy point, about which buzzards were circling.

"There is just one bush of rhododendron up there," he went on. "I saw it looking down from the Point last spring. I imagine it must blossom earlier than that across there on Bee Rock, being always in the sun. No, it's not budding yet," he added, with his eye to the glass. "You see that ledge just to the left? I dropped a big rock from the Point square on a rattler who was sunning himself there last spring. I can see a foothold all the way up the cliff. It can be done," he concluded, in a tone that made me turn sharply upon him.

"Do you really mean to climb up there?" I asked, harshly.

"If it blossoms first up there—I'll get it where it blooms first." In a moment I was angry and half sick with suspicion, for I knew his obstinacy; and then began what I am half ashamed to tell.

Every day thereafter Grayson took that glass with him, and I went along to humor him. I watched Bee Rock, and he that one bush at the throat of the peak—neither of us talking over the matter again. It was uncanny, that rivalry—sun and wind in one spot, sun and wind in another—Nature herself casting the fate of a half-crazed fool with a flower. It was utterly absurd,

but I got nervous over it — apprehen-
sive, dismal.

A week later it rained for two days,
and the water was high. The next
day the sun shone, and that afternoon
Grayson smiled, looking through the
glass, and handed it to me. I knew
what I should see. One purple cluster,
full blown, was shaking in the wind.
Grayson was leaning back in a dream
when I let the glass down. A cool
breath from the woods behind us
brought the odor of roots and of black
earth; up in the leaves and sunlight
somewhere a wood-thrush was sing-
ing, and I saw in Grayson's face what
I had not seen for a long time, and
that was peace — the peace of stub-
born purpose. He did not come
for me the next day, nor the next;

but the next he did, earlier than
usual.

"I am going to get that rhododendron," he said. "I have been half-way
up—it can be reached." So had I been
half-way up. With nerve and agility
the flower could be got, and both these
Grayson had. If he had wanted to
climb up there and drop, he could have
done it alone, and he would have known
that I should have found him. Grayson was testing himself again, and, angry
with him for the absurdity of the thing
and with myself for humoring it, but
still not sure of him, I picked up my hat
and went. I swore to myself silently
that it was the last time I should pay
any heed to his whims. I believed this
would be the last. The affair with the
girl was over. The flower sent, I knew

Grayson would never mention her name again.

Nature was radiant that afternoon. The mountains had the leafy luxuriance of June, and a rich, sunlit haze drowsed on them between the shadows starting out over the valley and the clouds so white that the blue of the sky looked dark. Two eagles shot across the mouth of the Gap as we neared it, and high beyond buzzards were sailing over Grayson's rhododendron.

I went up the ravine with him and I climbed up behind him — Grayson going very deliberately and whistling softly. He called down to me when he reached the shelf that looked half-way.

"You mustn't come any farther than this," he said. "Get out on that rock and I'll drop them down to you."

Then he jumped from the ledge and
caught the body of a small tree close
to the roots, and my heart sank at such
recklessness and all my fears rose again.
I scrambled hastily to the ledge, but I
could get no farther. I might possibly
make the jump he had made—but how
should I ever get back? How would
he? I called angrily after him now,
and he wouldn't answer me. I called
him a fool, a coward; I stamped the
ledge like a child—but Grayson kept
on, foot after hand, with stealthy cau-
tion, and the purple cluster nodding
down at him made my head whirl. I
had to lie down to keep from tumbling
from the ledge; and there on my side,
gripping a pine bush, I lay looking up
at him. He was close to the flowers
now, and just before he took the last

upward step he turned and looked
down that awful height with as calm a
face as though he could have dropped
and floated unhurt to the ravine be-
neath.

Then with his left hand he caught
the ledge to the left, strained up, and,
holding thus, reached out with his right.
The hand closed about the cluster, and
the twig was broken. Grayson gave a
great shout then. He turned his head
as though to drop them, and, that far
away, I heard the sibilant whir of rat-
tles. I saw a snake's crest within a
yard of his face, and, my God! I saw
Grayson loose his left hand to guard it!
The snake struck at his arm, and Grayson reeled and caught back once at the
ledge with his left hand. He caught
once, I say, to do him full justice; then,

without a word, he dropped — and I swear there was a smile on his face when he shot down past me into the trees.

I found him down there in the ravine with nearly every bone in his body crushed. His left arm was under him, and outstretched in his right hand was the shattered cluster, with every blossom gone but one. One white half of his face was unmarked, and on it was still the shadow of a smile. I think it meant more than that Grayson believed that he was near peace at last. It meant that Fate had done the deed for him and that he was glad. Whether he would have done it himself, I do not know; and that is why I say that though Grayson brought the flower

down—smiling from peak to ravine—
I do not know that he was not, after
all, a coward.

That night I wrote to the woman in
Kentucky. I told her that Grayson
had fallen from a cliff while climbing
for flowers; and that he was dead.
Along with these words, I sent a purple
rhododendron.

THE END